This Is the Day!

Written By **Nancy White Carlstrom**

Illustrated by **Richard Cowdrey**

ZONDERVAN.com/
AUTHORTRACKER
follow your favorite authors

For the Hall family: Nadine and Dave, Jessie,
Jacob, and Katie and Kaye Marshall—with love
–*N.W.C.*

(I) Give thanks to the Lord, for He is good.
His love endures forever.
–*R.C.*

ZONDERkidz

This Is the Day!
Copyright © 2009 by Nancy White Carlstrom
Illustrations copyright © 2009 by Richard Cowdrey

Requests for information should be addressed to:
Zonderkidz, Grand Rapids, Michigan 49530

Library of Congress Cataloging-in-Publication Data
Carlstrom, Nancy White.
　　This is the day / by Nancy White Carlstrom ; illustrations by Richard Cowdrey.
　　　　p. cm.
Summary: Celebrates the world of nature that God has made, from the raven's call
to a pod of orca whales.
　　ISBN 978-0-310-71428-6 (jacketed hardcover)
　　[1. Nature—Fiction. 2. Christian life—Fiction.] I. Cowdrey, Richard, ill. II. Title.
PZ7.C21684Th 2009
[E]—dc22
　　　　　　　　　　　　　　　　　　　2007003751

Art direction: Merit Alderink & Jody Langley
Design: Jody Langley

Printed in China

09 10 11 12 • 5 4 3 2

This is the day the Lord has made;
let us rejoice and be glad in it.

—PSALM 118:24

Monday

This is the day the Lord has made.

Tiptoe out into the morning world
    and stretch like the deer
    reaching for an apple
    high on the golden tree.

Skip through the dew diamonds
    glistening on the lawn
    where the quail feed.

Tuesday

Clap your hands and celebrate all of God's creation!

Sniff the garden's sweet rose,
  and your nose might meet a tiny tree frog.

Clap for the river otter who flaps in water
  but waddles across the grass
  through cottonwood fuzz,
  finding his way from the pond to the bay.

Wednesday

**Give thanks for all good gifts
this singing week brings.**

An eaglet learns to fly.

A red fox crosses the field
where rabbits stand like statues.
And in the distance a great blue heron
reaches beak-first across the wideness
   of the sky.

So give thanks.

Thursday

Hum your praise with the buzzing bees.

Walk gently under the robin's nest
and follow the butterflies
from bush to bush.

Get down on your knees.
The ladybug
climbs the stem of a cornflower,
and beetles run in circles
when you lift the rock.

Friday

Sing your own special song. You were created for this.

Call out cloud shapes the sky has made
   and watch light
     walk across the water.

Come back to shore and search for pebbles
   and beach glass.
     Write your name in the sand.

Saturday

Lift up your prayers with all God's creatures.

Join the song of the yellow warbler,
    the bark of the harbor seal,
    the raucous talk of ravens, and
    creature prayers rising from the mist—up, up, up.

Sunday

This is the day the Lord has made.

Celebrate
with a picnic supper
by the lighthouse.

A super pod of orca whales
has been invited ...
and here they come!
Breaching,
spy hopping,
clicking,
whistling,
calling,
spraying their praise.

Let all creation lift its voice.
This is the day the Lord has made.

Rejoice!
Rejoice!